The Adventures Collection

A Trio of Very Sexy Erotic Stories

M.C. Plains

Contents

He's getting a sexy birthday surprise

A Gift for my Husband

An erotic FFM short
M.C. Plains

A Gift for My Husband

It was about to be my husband's birthday, and I was determined to give him a gift he'd never forget. He was a wonderful husband; hot, sexy, smart and loyal. He was also very sexual, and extremely openminded. Fortunately for both of us, so was I. Very few things were off limits.

We'd fooled around with sexy singles before—usually women, although men weren't strictly off the table—but it had always been planned at least a few weeks in advance. The location, how it would happen - steamy hookup app, bar, club. We'd sit down over a cocktail and map out every piece of the evening, down to what we'd wear to seduce our... enjoyment for the evening.

But for my husband's birthday this year, I wanted to surprise him. No planning - on his part anyway; plenty on mine. Whoever I selected had to be just perfect. It was time for me to do some hunting, to find a woman to fuck my husband.

I was so excited by my idea that later the day I came up with it I launched at my husband on his arrival home. We made passionate love, right there on the floor beside the front door. He hadn't even had a chance to take off his suit. By the time we were done, it was fully removed and he was ready to change into something more comfortable. 'Wow, what's gotten into you? I'm not complaining—just, wow.' He said in amazement. He had no idea of the grand plan I had that had worked me into a frenzy just thinking about it.

I flicked through a few apps, and landed on someone that I couldn't take my own eyes off. Kimberly, it said her name was. 24. She had sandy blonde hair that hung in waves around her shoulders, and had big blue eyes with full, voluptuous lips. She had a variety of face-only and full-length pictures on her dating app profile and looked amazing from every angle. As I gazed at her gorgeous form, I realized there were some other angles on her that I wouldn't mind seeing.

I enjoyed exploring women as much as my husband did, and he really loved women. For me, I was aroused by their smoothness, their soft lines. Breasts were well, and fun to play with. I enjoyed the wetness and the very specific feeling and taste of a woman, and I enjoyed running my hands in between their legs and sliding my fingers and tongue inside them. I also enjoyed them returning the favor, seeing their long hair while my legs wrapped around their neck. It was fortunate that my husband and I had such similar interests in this department, and that we enjoyed sharing with each other.

I messaged Kimberly, introducing myself, and it wasn't long until she replied back to me. We arranged to meet for a coffee later that day at a nearby coffee shop. I dressed nicely, in smart casual, and spent a little extra time on my hair and makeup. While she was going to be a gift for my husband if I was honest about things she was also a big gift for me as well.

I enjoyed watching my husband fuck other women. It was like seeing him fuck me, but from so many different angles I couldn't see when I was involved directly. I got to see his large cock pleasuring someone else. I'd be lying if I didn't say there was a little bit of jealousy sometimes, but that seemed to ignite a deeper passion inside me, fueling me into a frenzy and making me throb with desire. And I was always involved. He would make sure I was taken care of, one way or another.

He also enjoyed watching me be fucked by another man. Sometimes he would join in, but he got an immense amount of pleasure from watching me be used by muscular, hot men who would plow me from all angles. He particularly liked it when they made me orgasm with their tongues. But this was his show, his birthday, and I felt like it was only proper for him to be more involved and to do more of the fucking and less of the watching. I intended to watch, and also substantially join in. Gosh, it was almost as fun thinking about and planning and anticipating his birthday than the amazing day his birthday was likely to be.

Kimberly looked just as good in person as she did on the app, if not better. She had charismatic energy about her, and we found plenty of things to talk about - the weather, what was going on in our neighborhood, our shared love of trashy TV. Her laugh was like one of those chimes that reverberates in the wind, slightly husky. She was very sexy, and I could tell she would be the one. After a while, we talked more in detail about my plans for her to be my husband's gift. I told her about what he liked, and what I liked, and she was very interested.

The plan was for her to come around to the house when he wasn't expecting it. I would hide her somewhere comfortable inside the house until I was ready for the surprise to be unleashed. This wouldn't be difficult; we had a very comfortable spare bedroom that was rarely used unless friends or family were visiting overseas, and he had no real reason to go in there. So I would smuggle her in, and she would get ready in the spare room. While she was doing that, I would plan to keep him distracted and prepare him for what was about to happen; for receiving his gift. We decided that it would be to all of our likings if there was substantial foreplay involved, because the anticipation of the actual acts that were going to happen were a big party of this real-life fantasy come true. We were going to involve some light BDSM. There would be some light spanking, some blindfolds, some tying up. And there would be lots and lots of licking and sucking and coming. It was a joy to hear how open she was to exploring us and letting us explore every inch of her. My husband was going to be so pleased by his surprise, fucking this beautiful and sexy woman.

By the end of our coffee, we were both in agreement that she would participate and become my husband's birthday gift. You could say that the three of us had a lot in common when it came to our wants, our needs, and our desires. We were also both very turned on, and decided to go and sit in her car for a bit, to let off some steam.

Luckily, she had parked in a shadowy corner of the parking lot where there wasn't too much traffic passing by. She joked that she'd parked here just in case, and we both laughed. She entered via her driver's door and I hopped in the passenger side. A moment later, we were making out. I ran my hands over her full breasts and she sighed with pleasure. I slid my hands under her shirt and up to the top of her bra, scooping down to get a handful of her breast, and tweaking her nipple. She moaned. She reciprocated by sliding her hand up my skirt, feeling how excited I was by our little rendezvous. We played with each other, kissing, fingering, and stopped short of using our tongues given our questionable location. We used our fingers to bring each other to orgasm. Both breathing heavily, we kissed once more, I straightened up my outfit although I still probably looked a bit ruffled, kissed her one more time, and left. She texted me and by the time I returned to my own car I had a text from her. *Can't wait to see you again, and to meet your husband xx.* I smiled. I had done something good, today.

When I got home, my husband noticed me smiling and humming tunes to myself as I pottered around making dinner and tidying up. He asked me what was going on and I refused to tell him. 'You'll find out soon,' I said. 'Okay, well you just seem really happy. I don't think I've heard you sing to yourself in quite a while. It must be something very good.'

'Oh yes it is, a very good thing. I can't tell you any more than that right now, but I think you'll be quite pleased.'

He probably thought I'd found a discount on bulk meat at the grocery store, or found a new purse at the mall. He had no idea what was about to come his way, literally.

Kimberly and I continued to text every now and then for the next week, leading up to the big day when my plan would come to fruition. She texted a few pictures of herself and some lingerie options, and I helped her to pick out what I thought my husband would find the sexiest. I'd be lying if I didn't admit that I saved the pictures in my phone and spent a fair amount of time looking at them, occasionally touching myself why I did so. Fuck, she was incredibly sexy. I couldn't get enough. The lingerie we settled on her wearing when she became a gift for my husband's birthday happened to also be what I thought would look best on her; skimpy but delicate, sexy yet also pretty. Just like her.

Finally, the day arrived. My husband and I slept in a little and I brought him coffee in bed. He had an enjoyable morning and early afternoon, relaxing around the house which is how he'd wanted to spend the day. He knew we'd likely be doing something in the afternoon or evening, but that was it, and he didn't ask too many questions. Typically, I'd bake him a cake and we'd go out for dinner. Sometimes I'd cook for him and we'd watch movies and have ice cream. Birthdays were always a fun day but never a giant event filled with elaborate plans, so he had no frame of reference for the pleasure I had planned for him today. He was going to be extremely surprised, and that was part of the fun. I like giving things to people that they want, when they're not expecting it. A true surprise that is very well-received and meets a real need.. or in this case, a real want and desire. That's when it's the most enjoyable.

While he happened to be napping on the couch, Kimberly arrived, and I quietly escorted her into the spare room. She gave me a sneak peek of her lingerie that we'd agree she would wear to further titillate my husband, although I felt pretty confident she wouldn't have it on for long.

We usually engaged in some type of intimacy on our birthdays–that was somewhat of a given–so he didn't question things when I pulled him off the couch and led him into the bedroom, where I secured his hands to the bedposts with thick, satin ribbons, and used one of his ties over his eyes like a blindfold. 'We haven't done this for a while,' he said. And it was true. We'd played around with tying each other up, but that had been years ago. And while our sex life could not be described as boring by any means, this just wasn't an area we'd chosen to explore in some time. I figured this would be a nice touch, a veritable bow on top of the gift I was about to give him. Something to ensure he would always remember this day, this experience, that I had so carefully planned.

I told him I'd be right back. I headed into the spare room where she had been waiting patiently. When I returned to her, she was sitting comfortably, reading one of several books that had been stacked on the dresser. She heard me come in and looked up from the book. 'Are you ready for me?' She asked with a big smile and sparkling eyes. She was breathtaking, and so very, very sexy. My husband was a very lucky man, and I was also a lucky woman. This was going to be fun. I licked my lips in anticipation. 'Yes, we're very ready for you. Well, my husband will be when he sees you. Of course, he doesn't know that you're going to be his sexy surprise.' I took her by the hand and led her out of the spare room, towards the bedroom door where my husband sat on the bed, tied up and blindfolded, not knowing what was about to happen.

I led her into the bedroom by hand, where I had tied my husband's hands to the bedposts. He was still blindfolded, and he couldn't see this sexy beauty that I'd brought inside. 'I'm back,' I said. 'And I have a surprise for you.' I put my finger over my mouth, signaling to her to be quiet as we slowly approached the bed. 'Oh yeah?' He asked, not having a clue what was going on. For all he knew, I'd baked him a cake, got him a watch in a gift box, and maybe purchased some massage oil if I was feeling frisky. But tonight, he was about to have a very sexy, very much alive, surprise. My husband was going to have the time of his life with this sexy woman I had found for us.

I climbed onto the bed and then kissed him on the mouth. He kissed me back. Our tongues explored each other's mouths, heat intensifying between us. I pulled away and gestured for her to go in and do the same. I watched as she sat on the edge of the bed, just as I had done, and leaned over bringing her mouth to his. Again, he kissed back. After a moment, he appeared to realize that her lips felt different, her tongue, no doubt her scent. 'Oh, and what do we have here?' He asked, interest clear in his voice. I hopped on the other side of the bed and said 'I told you, I brought you a gift. Wanna see?' He nodded and I slipped the blindfold from his eyes. 'Oh my,' he said, looking her up and down as she sat beside him in her tiny lacy lingerie. His eyes trailed over her face, her throat, her full breasts and lower down. 'Did I do good?' 'Oh you did very good,' he said, licking his lips.

I reached over to him again, putting my mouth to his and kissing him, tongues once again exploring. My hand also explored and there was more than a gentle stirring happening in his pants. I encouraged her to lean over towards me and I kissed her as well. He watched as we made out in front of him. I reached out and fondled her breast through her bra and he was clearly extremely turned on. I could see that he was as hard as stone now. She leaned towards him and kissed him as well, tongues intertwined, and her hand slid down towards his girth. 'Mmm,' she moaned as she rubbed him through his pants. Together, we pulled down his underpants and his rock hard cock unfurled, immediately standing at attention.

We slid down his body and kissed it together, along its length, on either side while he watched. 'Oh god that feels so fucking good,' he said. 'There's a buy-in before we'll untie you. You know what you have to do.' He smiled. 'I'm down for that. Take the rest of your clothes off and come here. Put your pussy on my face,' he told her. She complied, her bra and panties sliding off into a pile on the floor. She climbed back onto the bed and stood over him. His hands still tied to the bedposts, he tilted his head up and she leaned so that her pussy met his eager tongue. I watched with pleasure as I watched his tongue extend and lick her pussy and clit, up and down, up and down. She gyrated against him, gaining speed as he lapped at her. 'Oh fuck,' she said. 'You're right, he's good at this.' I'd filled her in previously about his enjoyment of performing oral and his skills in that area. 'Turn over and face the other way, put your ass in my face.' Again, she complied and he took his time licking her pussy and her ass, up and down, in and out. I loved watching him work from this angle, pleasuring this sexy woman until she came, squeezing herself hard against his face as she rode the wave of orgasm.

She immediately leaned forward and began to suck his cock which she'd had prime view of while he'd been licking her from behind. She enveloped him inside her mouth, and he thrust himself in and out. I could tell that he wanted to be untied, as he eyed her sweet ass in front of his face. He wanted to touch her, to hold her, to control her, and to do very naughty things to his birthday gift as well as to me. I walked over to each of his wrists and unbound him so that his hands were free. Now, the party could really get started.

'Come and ride my cock,' he growled. She lifted a leg over his muscular torso, straddling him. He lined her up against his rock hard cock and slid her on top of him, enveloping his girth with one firm thrust as he pulled her down. She cried out in pleasure, 'oh fuck, you're huge!' And he did have a sizeable one, that's for sure. Being that she was incredibly wet, soaking even, that wasn't an issue. I watched as he bounced her up and down on his hard cock, her breasts jiggling in multiple directions as she rode him.

I enjoyed watching her pussy slide over his hard dick, over and over again, both of them clearly enjoying themselves, just like I was.

'Get over here,' he directed me. 'Sit on my face, facing her.' Who could resist that type of directive? Compliantly, I went to the bed and hopped atop, near the pillows. I turned around, so that the headboard was to my back, and climbed aboard his face. I could feel his sweat, mixing with mine. He reached out his tongue and lapped at me. I was also very wet, and he ran his tongue around my lips and then plunged it inside me.

She continued to bob up and down on his cock, and I reached out and fondled her perky breasts as they bounced, enjoying the feel of their weight in my hands. I tweaked her nippled firmly and they became even more erect as she kept riding my husband.

I also continued to ride his face, ensuring my clit brushed against his facial stubble, stimulating me and causing ripples of pleasure to radiate throughout my lower body.

I felt him push me off him, and he moved me aside. 'Turn over and turn around, on your hands and knees. Side by side, facing away from me.'

We both did as he instructed.

He pulled out a paddle from behind the bed and sparked me firmly. I cried out in pleasure. He did the same to Melody and she squealed in enjoyment. 'I see that you both like to be spanked,' he said, clearly pleased. 'Time for me to fuck you both at the same time.'

He slid into me firmly and thrust a few times. My pussy surrounded his girthy cock, and the sensation as he slid in and out of me was magical. Then without warning, he pulled out and I heard her moan in pleasure as he ended her, thrusting several times. He continued to alternate, sharing his big dick between our two welcoming pussies. He would grab my hips as he rammed into me, occasionally pulling my hair which sent pleasant shivers over my neck and down my back. Melody and I were both breathing heavily, and from time to time we would look over and smile, occasionally stealing a sweet tongue kiss. 'Oh yeah, kiss each other while I fuck both of you, you're so sexy to watch.'

'Lay on your back, I want to fuck her while she eats you out.'

Again, no complaints there. I lay down on my back and she climbed forward on her hands and knees and brought her voluptuous lips to my pussy, kissing along the lips and then sticking her tongue out to tease my clit. I watched as he entered her from behind, making eye contact with me the whole time. She moaned when he did, causing her lips and tongue to vibrate on my pussy.

She stuck her tongue inside me and thrust it in and out in the same rhythm with which he was fucking her. I was incredibly worked up, excited to watch my husband fuck this sexy young woman while she devoured my throbbing, wet pussy.

She returned to focus on my clit, making fervent circles. I grabbed her head, pulling her against me as I rode her face to orgasm. She kept licking the entire time, sending further sparks of pleasure from my pussy to my entire body.

The sight of me orgasming from the tongue of this attractive young woman was enough to send my husband over the edge himself, and I watched as he closed his eyes and slammed into her, grabbing her hips and holding her firmly as he came inside of her. They slowly rocked to a standstill, and he pulled out of her, turning to rest on his back. 'Come here, ladies,' he said, gesturing to either side of him. He put his arms around each of us and we snuggled into his arms, smiling. It was relaxing, lying there satisfied and in the companionship of another sexy female.

After a little while, we fell asleep and napped, both of us still in his arms. When we woke, we lazily disentangled ourselves and Kimberly went into the spare room to dress. We met her near the front entrance. 'We must do this again sometimes. I know regifting is taboo, but I really would like to regift your present to you again. If that's okay with both of you.'

Kimberly leaned in and kissed me first, slowly with her tongue, and then leaned over to my husband who reciprocated eagerly.

'Fine with me, I would be pleased to be a gift for both of you, any time you want.'

'More than fine with me as well,' said my husband. He slapped her ass as she walked out the door.

It wasn't long since Kimberly had left my house when my husband found me in the kitchen. He leant up against me and I felt his hard dick pressing against my back. He hoisted my pants down and slid into me, proceeding to fuck me hard against the countertop without saying a word. He was rough and silent until he came. He moaned in pleasure, coming inside me as he wrapped his muscular arms around me and held me tight against him. 'Oh god, I love you so much. You might be the perfect wife. Thank you for my birthday present.' He left to go have a shower. I knew this would be one of many follow-up sessions to continue, and that I had selected the perfect give that would keep on giving. Whether or not we saw Kimberly again–and that was certainly not off the table–I knew I would be benefiting from this day for a long time to come.

THE END

"A delectable lesbian romp"

An erotic lesbian getaway
to remember

A Weekend
with my
Girlfriends

M.C. Plains

A Weekend with My Girlfriends

EVER SINCE WE'D BEEN married, my husband liked to send me off on women's weekends with a few of my closest friends. He insisted upon it. He would put us up in a nice rented house, usually somewhere secluded in the mountains or by a lake. Somewhere that we could really let loose and get away from it all. He would hire in specialists to take care of us.

It wasn't entirely selfless on my husband's part, though; he got something out of the arrangement as well. One of the rules we had in our relationship is that twice a year, he was always able to do what he wanted, to step outside of our relationship and indulge his own fantasies. But perhaps that's a story for another time. We'll see.

On this occasion, he had rented a 3 bedroom home tucked away into the mountains in a small resort town. There were five of us, so most of us would have to share a room with another person, but that usually ended up happening naturally anyway so everyone was okay with the arrangement. The town itself had just the basics needed when on a vacation like hours—a convenience store and a small restaurant were located a short five minute drive away. But most of what we needed at our getaway destination was already there. He'd of course phoned ahead and ensured that the kitchen was already fully packed with the finest wines, cheeses, charcuterie, and a fair amount of fresh meats, produce and other items that meant we could cook for each other without needing to leave. This was useful, as we generally wanted to maximise the time we had in these beautiful locations that he would pick out for us.

My friends were all incredibly attractive women in their own ways. It's not that I went for a certain type of aesthetic when it came to friends—I don't think that most people do—but I certainly ended up with a group on this trip that exuded confidence in their bodies, and in each other. This entire group had gotten together on this type of outing before, except for Mandy who was new. I had met her in a book club and we had been drawn to each other. She was cute, with cropped blonde hair and a taut body with perky breasts; she was funny, kind, and also seemed open-minded. That was an essential quality when it came to inviting people on these trips. After a few coffee dates, I'd casually mentioned this trip to Mandy to gauge initial interest, and she had immediately picked up on my queues. I hadn't needed to explain to her in great detail; she seemed keen on the idea of spending the weekend with a group of women who I could personally vouch for as being worth spending a few days with. I also got the sense that I wasn't going to explain to her what occurred on these cherished trips beyond the surface level. While I had told her about the spas, the food, the movies and the banter, it seemed obvious to her that in addition to the regular stuff you'd expect, we were also going to spend more quality time together. And she seemed very open to that. I may have shared a snippet with her, of course, more to tantalise her further rather than because I didn't think she knew what to expect. And that seemed to go down well. So well, in fact, that we would leave those conversations feeling hungry. A few sexy pictures had been exchanged in the process, a caress of the thigh or gentle brush of the side of the breast as we sat closely to each other on our coffee dates. I think both of us were just incredibly excited to explore each other more intimately—but we both held to a certain level of what we considered propriety, and didn't let things get any further until our activities would fall under the official auspices of the women's weekend, where as far as I was concerned, anything goes.

The group text always seemed to heat up in the week's leading up to the women's retreat as well. The other women—Cassandra, Yvette and Rebecca—were excited that I was bringing a new friend along. We would occasionally invite new people along, always well-vetted by someone in this trusted group. Some would just be invited for the one trip, while others—like Cassandra, who Yvette had first introduced to the group, became a staple part of our circle and would be invited as a central part of every trip thereon. There was always a huge sense of anticipation before each women's retreat. We would text about what we were bringing, and share information about the holiday home itself so we would be intimately familiar with what each destination had to offer. Occasionally, one of us would do some light research about the local area—more out of general interest than anything serious; we all knew that we weren't likely to leave the vacation home much if at all. It also helped us to answer basic questions when friends or colleagues knew we were going away on a women's retreat. It's not like it would be appropriate for us to share what really went on on these trips.

Keeping this a secret, firmly under wraps, was part of the allure. But the real attraction was the opportunity to spend quality time with these gorgeous women. To engage in activities that weren't part of our regular, day-to-day lives. As I packed my things, ensuring to bring items of clothing and skincare—including a deliciously scented moisturiser that I liked to slather all over my body—that made me feel confident, sexy, gorgeous, I reflected on how lucky I was to be able to do this several times a year. I truly had the best husband.

We enjoyed a lazy breakfast of fresh fruits, yogurt, granola, pastries and of course mimosas, expertly prepared by my friend Madeline. While not a complex meal in itself, with most items premade, she always managed to set everything out on the kitchen island in a way that looked like it was straight out of the pages of an interior design or cooking magazine created by a food artist. Over pain au chocolate and cappuccinos, we chitchatted about what was going on in our lives. Husbands, kids, work—everything was so hectic these days, and while we intended to send more texts to our group chat like we used to, time tended to rush by meaning that we had more to catch up on than originally intended. We usually spent the first morning of our trip in this way; while we did truly enjoy catching up with each other and hearing what was going on in everybody's lives, there were other things this type of trip entailed once these niceties had gotten out of the way. We were there for fun, and deeper friendship connections of a sort that not all friends engaged in. It's one of the main reasons why we were only too happy to keep returning to these all-expenses-paid vacations that my husband insisted upon, several times per year.

He had booked a team of spa therapists, who greeted us after our lazy breakfast on the first morning. They arrived at the door, all immaculately dressed in their spa technicians outfits. We were pampered from head to toe—facials, body scrubs, massages, manicures, pedicures leaving us polished and glowing in relaxation. After several hours of this decadent pampering, we tipped the spa team generously and they left. It was around this point in the trip that we generally turned our attention to our own self-initiated displays of personal attention.

We got into the hot tub and enjoyed the steam rising up into the cool air. The layout of the hot tub meant that I needed to sit close to Cassandra. I smile at her, the hot water pooling around her milky shoulders, her hair floating around her in the moonlight. She looked radiant, like a moon goddess. The top of her breasts floated atop the water, and even with the jets on I could see that her nipples were hard. We leaned towards each other and kissed, her lips soft and voluminous against my own. Gentle at first, we explored each other's mouths, and our interlock quickly became more passionate. It wasn't the first time that Cassandra and I had made out, and our mouths took naturally to one another, like old friends—like us.

While I had my eyes closed as we continued to kiss, I felt somebody float over in the hot tub towards us and it was our newcomer, Mandy. Her blonde hair was cropped beneath her chin and remained out of the water. The tops of her perky breasts also floated, just submerged. 'May I join you?' She asked, almost shyly but the lust and intention were clearly there. 'Of course you can,' and we welcome here over. Tentatively, she reached towards me and pulled me into a kiss, her tongue exploring mine; Cassandra reached in as well. This makeout session had become a triangle and we were all only too happy to have a third in our embrace. Cassandra reached out and touched one of Mandy's gorgeous breasts, and I also extended my arm to caress the other. Her nipples were hard, too. She moaned and smiled lazily. We alternated for a while, massaging each others breasts, grabbing their soft flesh in our hands and tweaking each other's nipples lustily. Cassandra took one of mine in her mouth and sucked on my nipple, gently nibbling at it from time to time. Pleasure radiated from my nipple down to my groin which was throbbing with excitement by this point.

'Should we initiate her?' Glancing in Mandy's direction, I asked Cassandra, eager to keep things progressing. 'Yes, I think it's time,' she agreed. We directed Mandy to sit on the edge of the spa, and she obeyed, following our directions to climb up and sit so that only her feet were submerged in the water. I took the lead in spreading her legs apart. 'Welcome to our women's retreat, Mandy,' I said. I reached my face towards her, and extended my tongue, teasing her labia gently at first. I spread apart her pussy lips and my tongue tickled at her pussy, again, gently. I flicked it up towards her clit and she moaned. 'We like to share around here, if that's okay with you.' She nodded hungrily. The other women formed a line, Cassandra first. I moved to the side and Cassandra moved in, where I watched as she too hungrily extended her tongue and lapped at Mandy's pussy, teasing and swirling it, up and down. Mandy's hips swayed in rhythm to Cassandra's expert licking. Cassandra extended two fingers and inserted them into Mandy's now very-wet pussy while she continued to sick, clamping down on her clit and gently nibbling from time to time. Mandy was moaning with pleasure. Cassandra moved out of the way and then Rebecca was next, she too fondling Mandy's pussy with her fingers and her tongue, causing Mandy to cry out in pleasure. And finally Yvette took her turn. 'I'll finish her off, if that's alright with you ladies.' We all nodded and smiled, and Mandy looked on in anticipation.

Yvette twirled her tongue around Mandy's clit, and Mandy arched her back in enjoyment. Yvette formed her tongue into a hard, cylindrical shape and we could see that she began to tongue-fuck her; Mandy started to gently rock her hips against Yvette's hard tongue as it pleased her inner walls, reaching deeper within her. Yvette then returned her tongue's attention to Mandy's clit and started to penetrate her pussy with her fingers, in and out, while her tongue swirled around creating ripples of pleasure for Mandy. We all looked on, enjoying watching our new friends' pussy being pleasured by our long-time friends' tongue that we had felt on our own many times before. We knew how it felt to be on the receiving end from Yvette—and the giving end, for that matter. Mandy continued to moan, and her volume increased as she got closer to orgasm, finally cresting the wave and pulling Yvette's face hard onto her pussy as she came on her. 'Good girl,' we all nodded and encouraged Mandy as she sat back, satisfied, looking at us all in both excitement and almost disbelief, her legs still dangling over the side of the hot tub where we had all taken turns pleasuring her with our tongues. 'I'm glad I joined you on this trip,' she joked. 'So are we,' I said.

It was time to go inside at this point and we put on robes—not that we would be wearing them for long, and we retreated to the living room. It was luxurious, decadently spread with lush carpets and rugs. A fireplace crackled in the background, perpetuating the electric ambience that was already naturally circulating amongst the five of us. We poured champagne—five tall and elegant flutes—and several of us sat on the comfortable couch, Mandy and Cassandra opting to sit on the floor next to each other. Very quickly, we decided that it would be more fun to drop our robes and they sat in puddles of material around us. We preferred to sit near each other and allow our gaze to run down each other's feminine form. As we sipped on our champagne, relaxed by the fireplace, I felt lucky to be in the company of such lovely ladies. Ladies with whom my friendships extended beyond the platonic and into the more carnal.

Yvette got up after a while and exited the room, returning with a box. It was our box of pleasure, we would jokingly to refer to it; but the name was apt, as it contained all manner of dildos, vibrators and other sex toys, some light bondage items like handcuffs and wrist and ankle ties. Yvette appeared to have expanded our selection from the usual variety, which was so like her, helping to ensure that each of our getaways was more adventurous, even more exciting than the last.

'Why don't you put on a bit of a show for us, Yvette and Rebecca? You've been hot for each other all trip so far, I've seen those looks. You can't wait to fuck. And I want to watch. I'm sure the other ladies do as well.' Cassandra and Mandy both nodded. 'So why don't you get started and then we'll join you, but first a bit of exhibitionism from you both, just the way you like it.' It as true—we'd got to know over the years that if there's anything Yvette and Rebecca enjoyed, it was an audience while they fucked. And they had formed a special connection that was unique to them. They were both incredibly sexy women, and were seemingly drawn to each other's confidence in their own body's, and had developed an insatiable yearning for each other. At times, it had created some sentiment of jealousy amongst the group, as they almost had their private subset of a relationship that was more in-tense than the broader collective. But it was also incredibly hot to watch them get it on together, so nobody had made a giant deal out of it.

Yvette grinned, and said to Rebecca, 'Shall we?' Producing a dildo from her box of magic tricks. Rebecca nodded, reaching out to tweak Yvette's nipple. She pushed Yvette towards the floor and Yvette got into a tabletop position on all fours, facing away from Rebecca. Cassandra, Mandy and I watched thirstily as we saw Rebecca extend her tongue, spreading Yvette's asscheeks apart and licking at her asshole, rimming her teasingly with her tongue. Yvette moaned. Rebecca continued to lick at her, swirling her tongue about her ass and then lowering it to her pussy where she tongue fucked her, in and out. Yvette swayed against her. Satisfied that Yvette was sufficiently wet and ready to be entered with something larger, Rebecca picked up the dildo. It was large and glistened in the light of the fireplace. She inserted it into Yvette, slowly at first, and then began thrusting it into her more firmly, the pace intensifying. Yvette rolled against it with her hips, enjoying being fucked by the dildo. It was pleasurable watching Rebecca ram the dildo into Yvette, who at some point decided that it was Rebecca's turn. She turned around as Rebecca pulled the dildo out of her pussy, and cleaned it with her tongue. 'Mmm, you taste wonderful, just like you always do,' Rebecca said appreciatively.

Yvette pulled a red silk ribbon out of the box and fastened Rebecca's wrists behind her, and pushed her back until she was lying on her back, unable to use her hands. Yvette pushed

Rebecca's legs apart and produced a strap-on from the box of pleasurable items and put it on. After teasing Rebecca with her tongue for a moment, just to get her even more excited, she leaned over Rebecca and inserted the dildo deep inside her. She was wet enough that she was able to take it deep and hard from the outset. Cassandra, Mary and I were at the edge of the couch seat by this point, lazily fingering ourselves as we watched Yvette fuck Rebecca with the strap-on. She thrusted in and out of Rebecca's pussy, which we could see tightly enveloped the large dildo. Rebecca was moaning and occasionally crying out in pleasure as she lay there, wrists restrained, while Yvette continue to plow her. They then decided to scissor, their pussies interlocked and their legs reaching behind each others backs as they rhythmically swayed against each other. Their clits were rubbing on each other, and by their facial expressions it was obvious that they were sending ripples of intense pleasure cascading throughout each other's interlinked bodies. I found myself entranced, envious of their ability to know exactly what the other was wanting, and very much wanting some similar pleasure of my own. I could see that the other ladies on the couch were equally as mesmerised, watching Rebecca and Yvette scissor their pussies together sensually.

'Alright ladies, I think it's time for us to join in. What do you think?' I eyed Cassandra and Mandy and reached out for both of their hands. I brought their index fingers that had been strumming against each of their clits into my mouth, sucking on them and getting to taste most women at the same time. They both nodded, and we climbed onto the floor to join Yvette and Rebecca. For the next however long it was—well into the night—the living room floor became a frenzy of tangled limbs. There were fingers and tongues inserted wherever they felt like exploring, licking and sucking. Dildos and vibrators plunging into pussies and assholes, thrusting rhythmically. Partners swapped and the entire group at times would find itself sprawled out over each other, hungrily. At one particular point in this frenzied orgy I found myself back with Cassandra—we naturally seemed to gravitate towards each other, too, and I inhaled the musky scent of her pussy. I licked at her hungrily, and rammed an especially large dildo into her; she liked them big, always had. She bucked against the dildo that I expertly helped in my hand, fucking her with this long and girthy tool of pleasure. I lay on top of her as I did so, our tongues exchanging space in each other's mouths, both of them tasting like the many women we had both pleasured orally this evening. I fucked her hard, all the way to orgasm, and she smiled—she could always count on me to bring her pleasure.

After the frenzied group sex was done, we all headed to bed. We only needed two beds really; Cassandra, Mandy and I shared one, and Rebecca and Yvette shared the other. I woke the next day to find myself sprawled between Cassandra and

Mandy. We all smelled like sex from the night before and it was wonderful, a musky and sweet scent reminding us of the carnal activities we'd engaged in together the night before. We snuggled against each other and I enjoyed lying in their arms, them lying in mine, as we rested. Their feminine energy had a beautiful quality that I was attracted to even when we weren't engaging in physical acts. We enjoyed an intimacy between us, a truly deep connection.

By the time we decided to lazily stretch and get out of bed, and have quick showers, Rebecca and Yvette had already risen and gotten ready. We found them downstairs, the scent of banana walnut pancakes and strong coffee pleasuring our nostrils as we reached the kitchen. 'You've been busy,' I said to Yvette and Rebecca. 'Oh yes, we certainly have,' said Rebecca, winking cheekily at Yvette. 'You indulged in more after last night?!' 'Maybe,' laughed Yvette coyly. 'You two are insatiable on these trips!' 'Maybe not just these trips, although this is where we do more of the group stuff,' said Yvette. Interesting. It sounded like their extracurricular activities had expanded beyond our twice-yearly vacations. I had always suspected this was more than a holiday fling for them. I was happy that this had turned into even more, even if it was only a sexual connection with a friendship attached.

The five of us enjoyed a feast of pancakes, waffles, fresh fruit, coffee and juice and we lounged around for the remainder of the trip. Each evening was spent indulging in a ritual of nakedness; our tongues continued to explore each other's bodies, getting to know every crevice and how to best pleasure the other. Mandy took a real liking to our trip and effectively formed a throuple-type arrangement with myself and Cassandra at times we found ourselves naturally migrating off into groups, and our bed is where she spent each night. But we made sure that she got some quality time with Rebecca and Yvette, too. After all, she was our newbie, our shiny new plaything.

When we left the mountain hideaway, we all kissed each other goodbye and gave each other long, deep hugs. We knew that we would be getting together again in a few months, and for all of us it was a highlight of our year. My husband gave me plenty to be thankful for, and I was going to be sure to find many ways to express my gratitude when I got back home.

'Did you have a nice women's retreat, dear?' My husband kissed me on the lips when I returned home. 'It was fantastic, just like always.' 'I'm so glad. I saw that Mandy seemed to fit right in. Glad that this was another great time.' He always made sure that the homes he rented had a very good camera setup, one that he could control remotely. It was part of why he was so keen for me and my friends to have access to these types of homes. It was all part of the fun, and it fulfilled his strong voyeuristic fantasies as much as my own female-on-female desires. A match made in heaven, some might say. My friends of course knew about this little element of their all-expenses-paid luxury trip and were fine with the arrangement, all things considered. 'In fact, why don't we watch some of the footage together, there are some parts that I'd like you to tell me about in more detail, maybe a bit of show and tell.' 'I'd be more than happy to,' I said. We cheers-ed our coffee mugs together. 'To women's weekend.' 'To women's weekend.' I could tell he was hard, ready for me.

THE END

Three was fun. Now she's
inviting a friend to join.

The Babysitter Brings a Friend

M.C. Plains

The Babysitter Brings a Friend

Recently, my husband and i had some fun with our babysitter, who was back from college for the holidays. Her name is Alyssa, and as my husband likes to describe her, she's a sexy little thing. Her firm yet curvy twenty-year-old body excited every inch of my husband and me; he and I have had many pleasurable experiences since, together and solo, thinking about that day. The thing with this type of delectable experience is that it's not just the day that you get to watch your husband fuck your babysitter that's hot; it ignites a spicy spark in your relationship that extends long past that.

On her way out the door she had casually mentioned that she might bring a friend of hers along next time. And today was 'next time'. Alyssa was bringing her friend, Ruby, around to babysit. While our first encounter with Alyssa gave us both plenty to think about, inspiring many exquisite nights of everything from gentle and tender lovemaking to fast, rough fucking, neither of us had been able to get what seemed to be a throwaway comment from Alyssa off our minds.

We didn't know anything about her friend at first; one day, as we chatted over dinner, I decided to raise the topic.

'Darling, you know how Alyssa mentioned maybe coming around again sometime.'

'How could I forget?' His gaze turned lusty, from the mere mention of Alyssa. I would have been jealous but I thought she was hot too, and it was even hotter watching my husband fucking her. It would have been hypocritical of me to complain when the mere thought of her made me want to touch myself.

'Well, I was thinking... I could text her and just put it back out there as an idea. Try to see if she was serious or if she was just making polite conversation.'

'Don't know if I'd call that polite,' said my husband, winking at me. 'But yes, I think you should investigate further.'

I didn't want to come on too strong, although by the way she'd behaved, confidently exploring every inch of my husband's body and my own, I didn't think she was one to be easily scared away. That said, I still wanted to be careful. I really wanted a repeat.

So I tried to be casual in my text. *Thinking about the last time you came round. Fancy a round 2?*

She didn't reply. Half an hour went past. I don't know why I was expecting her to respond immediately; she was a popular twenty-year-old woman and I'm sure she was out with her friends or working another 'real' babysitting gig, not sitting around waiting for me to text her. But as that first half hour crept by, and another one, I became increasingly concerned. *Shit,* I thought, *I've freaked her out. She's not going to reply.*

I was embarrassed, verging on mortified. In my mind, this was becoming one of those situations that was growing into something much bigger. I instinctively knew that but at the same time it was hard to quell the panic with all of the irrational thoughts flooding my mind. *What if she had a horrible time with us? What if she liked being with my husband but not me? What if, what if, what if?!* It was while I was in the shower in an attempt to calm and distract myself that I heard the phone ding. I leapt out of the shower as quickly as I could without taking a spill on the slick linoleum floor and grabbed the phone from the vanity. I breathed a sigh of relief as I saw that the message was from Alyssa. *I've been thinking about it as well. Meant what I said, I have a friend who'd be down to join us. Let me know if you're interested xx.*

I waited half an hour before I replied, again trying to be casual. *Sounds fun. Let's do it. Friday at 7? Kids are away this weekend with the grandparents, btw. Just you and your friend this time.* I was trying not to let on just how interested

I was, and how interested I knew that my husband would also be.

She immediately replied. It's a date. Will send a pic later xx.

What a great idea, a pic. It would be fun to show my husband exactly what we were going to be getting into, even though I might keep it to myself for a while first.

For the rest of the evening I acted like nothing was amiss. My husband didn't bring it up and neither did I, even though it was difficult to think about anything else.

Later that evening, while I was tidying up the kitchen and my husband was relaxing in the living room flicking between a sports game and a sitcom, my phone buzzed again. It was from Alyssa, and she had sent over a few photos of herself and her friend who was going to become our newest plaything.

I knew she was going to be cute, but I had no idea how cute. Alyssa's friend's name was Ruby, and they'd been friends for years. That's basically all I knew about her given the circumstances. But the photo revealed she was incredibly stunning in a sexy way. She had one of those knowing, cheeky gazes that always made you think a person was up to no good in the best kind of way. Good trouble, you might say. She had long hair and a gorgeous figure with ample breasts and a flat stomach, both of which she liked to show off in crop tops by the looks of the pics that Alyssa sent through. She also seemed fond of short shorts which revealed the very bottom of her asscheeks, perky and well rounded. Her face was incredibly attractive, piercing brown eyes and voluptuous lips that looked like they were made to do very naughty things. I couldn't wait to see them wrapped around my husband's cock, I thought, as I touched myself at the thought. Friday was going to be a very interesting night.

The rest of the week seemed to drag by like a snail. I busied myself with work and spent the after hours cooking and cleaning and reading. Anything to make time tick by so we could get closer to the weekend. My husband had been working late, and a few evenings during the week we'd enjoyed each other intimately. Our regular sex was good, if not a little vanille, especially when he was tired from work. I hadn't told him about Alyssa and her friend Ruby yet; I was trying to keep it a surprise until a couple of days before. I think he noticed that I seemed to be a little more energetic than normal, a bit fired up in the bedroom, but the difference wasn't enough for him to ask any questions. I was trying to meter things out a bit, pace it so that we still kept our desire for each other going, but in a way that ramped up towards Friday, and all that it entailed.

Over the first couple of days, I'd find myself occasionally going back to my photos where I'd downloaded and stored the pictures that Alyssa had sent through. While the photos could look perfectly innocent to a random bystander, I felt naughty looking at them. While Ruby and Alyssa were both fully clothed in each of them, I knew they wouldn't be come the weekend. Things were going to take a very naughty turn on Friday night, only a few more days to go.

By the time Wednesday rolled around, I couldn't keep it to myself any longer and I let him know that Alyssa would be coming over on Friday with her friend. I showed him the picture and I could tell he was into the proposition by the way his gaze turned lustful and his pants tightened. I took advantage of his horniness that evening, utilizing his girthy endowment all to myself. I knew, after all, that I was going to have to share on Friday. And I didn't mind at all, but I wanted extra dick time while it was available. A girl has needs, you see.

Finally, it was Friday. I made sure that I got some decent sleep the night before. It was so important that I was well rested for what was about to come. Conscious that I was going to be the oldest of the three women involved, I almost felt I had to prove myself, to not be the first to tire even though we were going to be expending a significant amount of energy. When I woke, I immediately realized that today was the day. I stretched, opting to take a yoga class to make sure I got any unnecessarily muscle kinks out. I smiled to myself during the yoga class; how ironic that I was getting these one out to explore more kinks later.

On Friday evening, I was freshly showered and had moisturized my body in a lather of delectable lotion that Alyssa had complimented last time, and appeared to have enjoyed licking off my body. I hoped that she would do it again, and that her friend might also want a taste. I wore a pretty but simple dress, that I knew I wouldn't be wearing for long. Underneath that, I was adorned in sexy, lacy black lingerie. I knew I was going to be the oldest woman in the room, but I still looked very good. I took care of my figure and I knew how to show it off. With my age also came wisdom and experience in the bedroom. These two ladies were quickly becoming experts in their sexuality, but there were still many things that they could learn from me.

When they arrived, I was reminded of just how sexy Alyssa was. She was wearing a very short skirt that showed off her amazing legs. A crop top exposed a hint of cleavage and a taut belly featuring a belly button piercing. Cute and sexy, just like her. She'd done her hair in pigtails, which might have seemed like a bit of a cliche–babysitter and all–but there were no kids to look after tonight, just the adults. And the whole look went together; again, cute and sexy, just like her. I enjoyed eyeing the way the light from the floor to ceiling windows illuminated her skin, causing her cleavage to glow welcomingly. I had an urge to bury my face between her breasts, but I kept it to myself for now. I was getting excited before things even began to heat up.

Ruby introduced herself and gave me a hug. I couldn't help but give her a once-over, looking at the full length of her body and taking it all in. She was wearing a similar outfit to Alyssa; a skirt and crop top. Must be the uniform amongst the twenty-year-olds these days, I thought to myself. Her breasts were perky, and I couldn't help but notice her nipples were hard under her top that stretched over her chest. Her hair hung loose in waves about her shoulders. As I welcomed them both in, I thought of how lucky my husband and I were to get to have these two sexy women as our playthings for the evening. I knew he would feel the same way the moment he got a glimpse.

My husband entered the room and he looked incredibly handsome, his short hair slightly tousled although no doubt not as tousled as it would be later. He wore a button up shirt and trousers, looking trendy and sophisticated. I could see both of the women eye him up as he came in and greeted the three of us. His eyes were drawn first to Alyssa, who he knew, and then to Ruby. He gave Alyssa a warm hug and a kiss on the cheek in greeting, and also gave Ruby a hug as Alyssa introduced them.

We sat down and made small talk. I noticed that my husband, too, was taking the time to take Alyssa in, piece by piece, glancing in her direction appreciatively. His eyes landed on her ample chest several times, and lowered to her short skirt. The way she was sitting on the couch meant that sitting across from her gave us both a little sneak peak at what lay underneath. Little lace panties that I looked forward to seeing on the floor pretty soon.

After chatting for a while, I could tell that the girls were interested in getting started. It was obvious by the way they were looking at each other as well as my husband. Alyssa had licked her lips a couple of times while speaking, and I saw my husband's eyes were drawn to her sexy mouth. Ruby also had a habit of biting her lip, which made me imagine the way her mouth would look latched onto a nipple, or other body part that she desired to nibble on.

There was an element of tonight which was entirely new to me. My husband had told me earlier, that he had decided part of tonight was going to involve me having to watch while he fucked these two very horny women. He wanted me to practice self-restraint but he knew I would only touch myself while I watched, so he took each of my wrists and secured them to the chair I sat in with shiny red satin ribbons. The girls then went and sat with him on the couch facing me, one on either side of him. He smiled sexily, he was the cat who got the cream. I looked on, helpless, but also filled with desire and anticipation at what I was about to watch.

He directed them to undress each other, and they began to kiss. They made out, holding each other's faces gently while they explored each other's mouths with their tongues, increasing in urgency as time went on. I felt a deep throbbing beginning between my legs, watching their tongues meander. Their hands began to discover each other's bodies, caressing each other's breasts. My husband directed them to remove each other's clothes, and they disrobed. Each pulled off the other's crop top and bra, leaving their beautiful breasts exposed. Two sets of hard nipples faced each other, rubbing against each other as the two women continued to make out. They kept their skirts and panties on for now.

Alyssa reached down and tugged on Ruby's nipples. Ruby moaned appreciatively. As if she'd read my mind earlier, Ruby then reached down and took Alyssa's hard nipple in between her lips, and tugged on it with her teeth, licking and sucking while Alyssa moaned with pleasure. Before long, they started to explore each other's lower areas with some gentle rubbing through each other's panties. When Alyssa reached her fingers inside Ruby's panties, my husband told them that was enough for now.

He had them lie down one beside the other, and he moved between the two, their legs spread wide apart. He licked each of them up and down, extremely slowly, and they both moaned with pleasure. My husband knew how to eat pussy, that's for sure. I watched his tongue dance across their lips, teasing their clits and sliding inside their pussies one back and forth, one after the other. They seemed to enjoy the tongue-fucking by the sounds they were making. I could see them make eye contact with each other as well as my husband as he inserted his tongue inside them. He then teased each of them, twirling his tongue over their clits fast, circular, in quick succession, once again back and forth, back and forth. He used his fingers, inserting two from each hand so that he was fingering both Alyssa and Ruby at the same time, alternating his mouth's attention between the two. By now, my own pussy was intensely throbbing and I had a strong urge to touch myself, but the restraints hold firm and I knew I had to be patient.

'Get over here and suck my cock,' my husband said, stopping what he was doing and demanding they pleasure him. He hadn't let either of them come yet, and wasn't intending to for a while. This was his show, and he liked to tease.

He sat down as he pulled his pants off, exposing a rock hard girthy cock that they both looked at with desire. They approached him and both got on his knees, moving their faces towards his erection. They licked and kissed all over his girth, and he groaned in pleasure as these two sexy goddesses pleasured him with their tongues.

I watched as Ruby and Alyssa took turns taking my husbands engorged cock in their mouths, deep throating him. He pulled on their ponytails as he thrust himself into their mouths, their voluptuous lips enveloping him. I was mesmerized watching as they went - in my 20s, I certainly didn't have skills like this.

He then said, 'Come here, Ruby. I want to see you more closely.'

He lay on his back and gestured for her to hop on the couch and straddle him. She complied, sitting on his face. He murmured in approval and began playing with her pussy and clit with his tongue. 'I want to tongue-fuck you,' and she nodded as if to say yes, please. I could see his tongue as it snaked up inside her. She then rode him as he focused his attention on her clit, and she seemed to enjoy sliding her clit against his stubble, until she came as he pulled her down against his mouth by her hips.

'Get on my cock, Alyssa,' he commanded. Alyssa also approached the couch and straddled him. 'God, you're such a sexy girl,' he said as she slid her pussy down onto him and began to bounce up and down on his cock, her breasts bouncing. I continued to sit and watch, mesmerised as my husband fucked two other women, both gorgeous, both much younger than me.

My husband continued to pleasure Ruby with his tongue, licking her up and down and side to side, occasionally slipping it completely inside of her, tasting her.

The whole time, Alyssa continued to ride him, slamming her pussy up and down hard on his cock, making a slapping sound as her ass hit his muscular quads.

'Get over there and pleasure my wife. She's waited long enough,' he said. Thank goodness, it was my turn. I felt like I was going to explode from the anticipation, watching him fuck these beauties while I sat helpless and restrained in the corner. I wanted to participate so badly, and was left aching with desire and no way to get rid of the pent-up feelings within me. But I had to stay tied up for now, it seemed. Both women approached me, and when they were close they both got on their knees and crawled towards me. Alyssa approached me first, and then Ruby. They kissed me on my mouth, both tasting like my husband, which I very much enjoyed. Then each took one of my nipples in their mouths and tugged at them with their teeth, at first very gently and then more roughly as I moaned with enjoyment. Sensations of pleasure rippled throughout my body; I loved it when my nipples got attention and they seemed to instinctively recognize it which made me very pleased. My husband watched on from the couch, looking very pleased with the sight before him, two gorgeous women pleasuring his wife.

Ruby then leaned down and started to pleasure me with her tongue. Alyssa soon joined in as well, and they would take turns flicking their tongues over my clit. Alyssa positioned herself slightly underneath me so she could focus on my pussy, sliding in and out while Alyssa continued to pleasure my clit. It wasn't long before the pleasure intensified and I found myself coming while they both had their faces pressed against me. I made eye contact with my husband as I rode the wave of an intense orgasm and he smiled at me, lust and something else in his eyes.

My husband came and untied me at that point and the four of us retreated to the bedroom. I was glad we'd opted for the California king sized bed that enabled all four of us to fit nicely in all sorts of positions as we fucked and sucked and bit and tugged and pulled and thrusted. Hands and mouths and other body parts rubbed against each other, my husband fucking all three of us with a passion and intensity that I hadn't seen before. He made all three of us come with his tongue and his cock, and we returned the favor several times. There was a little spanking, a bit of pinching, and some gentle nibbling; wherever the mood took us, and we all seemed to be on a similar page. After an incredible few hours of showering attention on one another, we all lay there spent, limbs dangling over each other's bodies, drenched in sweat and deeply satisfied.

Finally, it was time for the girls to leave.

We all put our clothes back on, and briefly adjusted our hair. To an innocent bystander we would probably have looked like some type of friendly group who just had a meal together. Which we did, of sorts.

Alyssa and Ruby, one after the other, approached me and gave me a hug and long kiss on the lips.

'Thank you for having us. We enjoyed visiting you.'

'We enjoyed having you. Very much.' I smiled at them, and so did my husband.

They picked up their bags and we saw them out. We could see them chatting excitedly as they headed out to the road to get their ride home.

My husband turned to me and said, 'I'm not finished with you. Get in here.'

He grabbed me and lifted me into the air, carrying me into the bedroom and throwing me onto the bed. I was delighted to find that he was still rock hard, and without waiting he ripped down my pants and plunged his girthy cock deep inside me. He thrust in and out of me, filling me up with his sizeable dick that he'd just shared with others, but now I was the only one it was interested in. He pounded me as I cried out in pleasure, enjoying the feeling of his cock slamming into my tight and hungry pussy over and over again until he came, shuddering on top of me.

'You're so fucking sexy. And today was really hot, don't get me wrong. I could fuck hot women like those two all day long. But you, you are the real deal. I'm so lucky to have you.'

'That might be the nicest thing you've ever said to me, you know that?' I felt warm, both from the pounding and also his kind words. I kissed him on his nose, smiled up at him, and then we both fell asleep, intertwined in each other's arms. I couldn't wait to see where this relationship took us next, but one thing was certain—nothing was off limits; as long as I was with him, I was up for anything.

THE END

Also By M.C. Plains

Join my newsletter for the latest info on new releases:
https://subscribepage.io/Gkj4yZ
Stack of Pleasure

https://www.amazon.com/dp/B0BCP5PSZP
It's my husband's fortieth birthday. So I'm giving him a very special gift - four sexy women, in a stack. He can do whatever he desires. And I will of course be joining in.

A Gift for My Husband

https://www.amazon.com/dp/B0BC2FJBKS
My husband's birthday is coming up really soon.
And this year, I'm planning a special surprise. She's very sexy, and she's going to be his special gift.

The Arrangements Collection: A Satisfying Trio of Sexy Stories

https://www.amazon.com/dp/B0BCDL7F4B

Tommy and his wife have a wonderful, cozy life together. But they also find dessert with Derek to be mutually satisfying. Marriage can lose its sparkle after a while, but their adult babysitter helps to bring it back.
Her husband always liked to watch. But it was time to invite a sexy stranger for dinner, and nothing was off the table tonight.

A Weekend with my Girlfriends

https://www.amazon.com/dp/B0BC6N89YL
My husband liked to book vacation homes for me and my closest girlfriends.
There, we would deepen our friendships on a whole new level.
This time, we're bringing a new friend, and she's going to join us for a sexy rendezvous. And we can't wait to initiate her.

The Hot Girl Summer Collection: A Trio of Sexy Stories

https://www.amazon.com/dp/B0BBS7G743
-A seemingly random encounter, as a sexy cowboy enters the ice cream shop. He's the last customer of the night.
-A tiki bar is a place that people go to escape. The customers tend to be more open-minded... about lots of things.
-A home cooking school where certain clients are invited to stay on for a little bit of fun after the lesson.

Inviting the Babysitter

https://www.amazon.com/dp/B0BBDCMMCX
Marriage can lose its sparkle after a while. She knows she's not the same as she used to be, especially after the kids. But she's determined to strengthen their marriage, starting in the bedroom. And it just so happens their babysitter is home from

college, and she's very, very sexy. She can tell her husband thinks so, too.

The Babysitter Brings a Friend

https://www.amazon.com/dp/B0BCH91JTB
Their babysitter has joined them before, and it was something they'll remember forever.
This time, she's bringing a friend.

Dinner for Three

https://www.amazon.com/dp/B0B9WGC45T
Tommy and his wife have a wonderful, cozy life together.

Ordering In

https://www.amazon.com/dp/B0BBNG631N
Her husband had always liked to watch. But now he wanted to get in on the action himself. It was time to invite a sexy stranger over for dinner. And nothing was off the table, tonight.

The Ice Cream Shop

https://www.amazon.com/dp/B09766NWKS
A seemingly random encounter, as a sexy cowboy enters the ice cream shop. He's the last customer of the night.
Ice cream isn't the only thing on the menu this evening.
It's going to be a long, hot summer.

Getting Freaky at the Tiki

https://www.amazon.com/dp/B0977QXF8X

People go to tiki bars to escape. That's why my husband and I find it easy to pick sexy strangers up there. I mean, we *are* a good-looking couple, which I'm sure makes things easier. But it's just like people at these types of places are more open-minded about... lots of things.

Recipe for Seduction

https://www.amazon.com/dp/B097HVFZVL
I run a cooking school out of my home kitchen. I have a large kitchen island which serves some unconventional purposes. Sometimes my clients are particularly attractive, and we invite them to stay on for a little bit of fun after the lesson. Today, one of those clients is stopping by. We're going to make a spiced apple pie, and we'll see what happens after that. I think it's going to be a fun time.